This book unfortunately belongs to:

_____

This book is dedicated to no one.

What did you expect from the Worst Love Book
in the Whole Entire World?

www.ackersbooks.com

Entire World Books: 4

All breathtaking and exhilarating illustrations and words created by Joey
Acker. All rights reserved. That means don't copy anything from this book.
The world can't handle this much beauty...

Copyright Joey and Melanie Acker 2020

Melanie was too blinded by love to help write this book.

ISBN-13: 978-1-951046-05-7

The WORST LOVE Book

in the Whole Entire World

Joey Acker

I love you.

There. I said it.

The end.

Right?

Of course not!

Because that would be GREAT! But no, I am STUCK in another one of these RIDICULOUS books!

I guess you want to know how a book above LOVE can be so bad?

Really?!?

Wouldn't you rather go read a nice
book about puppies or kitty cats?

Just go now. You won't hurt my feelings.

Seriously?

You're still reading this book?

Well that's just

LOVELY!

Reason #1: love stinks.

Oh yes. I said it.

Love stinks and you won't
EVER catch me falling in
LOVE!

NEVER

No way

NOPE

Cut it out

STOP

So let's just move on to
reason #2. Shall we?

Reason #2: there is a mushy
gushy poem in this book.

What does mushy gushy mean?

It means GROSS!

Roses are red.
Violets are blue.
You'll fall in love.
She'll be your boo.

YUCK!

I think I'm going to be sick...

Reason #3: there are flowers in this book.

Flowers SMELL funny.
Flowers do NOT live for a very long time.
Flowers, the fancy LOVE ones, cost a LOT of money.
Flowers HAVE to be taken care of, kind of like a dog, but they don't play with you.

And reason #4...

CHOMP   CHOMP

What is that noise?

It is I,
the Love
Goat.

Reason #4: this book is WEIRD.

I heard you're having a ba-a-a-d day!

I've had worse.
Why are you here?

I'm here to take you to your one true love!

How about NO.

How about

YES!!!

Reason #5: I've been
rocknapped!

Well, hello there!
I see the Love Goat brought
you.

What are you doing and why
am I in this cage??

I am making your LOVE POTION!

Reason #6: he has a
love potion and looks a
little crazy!

Hiyah!

You're welcome.

Ugh!
Isn't LOVE the
WORST?

Reason #7: I'm in LOVE!

Made in the USA
Monee, IL
19 January 2020